First published in Great Britain 2021 by Farshore
An imprint of HarperCollins*Publishers*
1 London Bridge Street, London SE1 9GF
www.farshore.co.uk

HarperCollins*Publishers*
1st Floor, Watermarque Building, Ringsend Road
Dublin 4, Ireland

Written by Serlina Boyd
Consultation and further text by Sue Omar
and Margot Rodway-Brown @naturalhairlocbar
Illustrations by Yabaewah Scott, ArtJaz, Allison Ferguson
Edited by Katrina Pallant
Designed by Andrea Philpots
Cover design by Pritty Ramjee and Jessica Coomber

Image credits: D and S Photography Archives/Alamy Images,
Zvereva Yana/Shutterstock.com, Artur Balytskyi/Shutterstock.com,
VectorShop/Shutterstock.com, Michel HUET/Contributor/Getty Images
Graphics: Shutterstock.com

ISBN 978 0 7555 0432 9
Printed in Great Britain by Bell and Bain Ltd, Glasgow
001

A CIP catalogue record for this title is available from the British Library.

Parental guidance is advised for all the hair tutorials within the book.

Stay safe online. Farshore is not responsible for content hosted by third parties.

Farshore takes its responsibility to the planet and its inhabitants very seriously.
We aim to use papers from well-managed forests run by responsible suppliers.

THIS BOOK BELONGS TO EVERY GIRL AND BOY WITH AWESOME, TEXTURED, BEAUTIFUL HAIR

In loving memory
of Auntie Min

CONTENTS

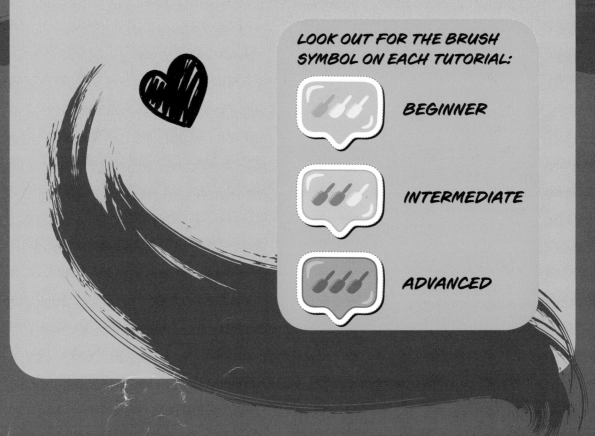

LOOK OUT FOR THE BRUSH
SYMBOL ON EACH TUTORIAL:

BEGINNER

INTERMEDIATE

ADVANCED

INTRODUCTION
FROM SERLINA & FAITH

AWESOME HAIR IS WHAT YOU HAVE AND DON'T YOU EVER FORGET IT!

Faith loves her hair and has been on an incredible journey into discovering the many things she can do with her AWESOME HAIR. A journey I wished I discovered as a young girl before using products to completely change my hair and its beautiful texture. I used to want hair like everyone else I saw on the TV and in magazines.

Cocoa Girl Awesome Hair is our book and we are so excited to celebrate your AWESOME HAIR with you. From our hair history to amazing styles and tutorials you won't be disappointed. I feel it is very important to do this book that focuses on Cocoa Girls and their beautiful hair because it has never been done before and it could be very instrumental in helping you look after your glorious curly crown.

"I'm a queen crowned in my curls"

WHAT YOU'LL NEED

Here are some tools and products that will help you create the styles in this book.

WATER SPRAY

WIDE-TOOTH COMB

TAIL COMB

FINE-TOOTH COMB

HAIR OIL

HAIR GEL

GEL

BOBBY PINS

ELASTIC BANDS

SMALL ELASTIC BANDS

SNAG-FREE HAIRBANDS

Use small black elastic bands to secure the ends of your braids. Always dip the bands in oil before applying to protect your natural hair.

HAIR CLIPS

SCRUNCHIES

BEADS

BEADS

GLITTER GEL AND APPLICATION BRUSH

HAIR FLOWERS

BLACK HAIR HISTORY

Hair is an important part of Black history. It shows our creativity and culture throughout the ages.

ANCIENT EGYPTIANS

Egyptians wore many different hairstyles that some people still wear today. They were the original trailblazers!

EGYPTIAN QUEEN

This is Nefertiti. She was an Egyptian queen who wore her hair in an amazing high-top crown!

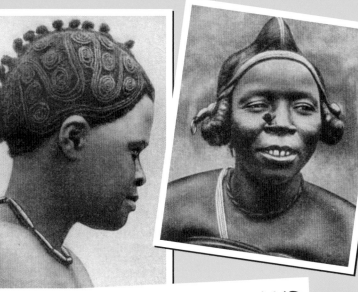

ANCIENT AFRICAN HAIR

Hair was so important in the culture of Ancient Africa. It could be used as a way to identify a person's age, wealth, religion, marital status, tribe and family background.

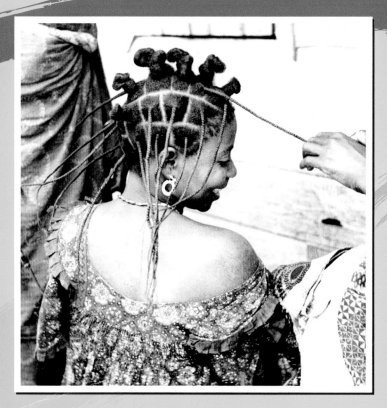

FAMILY AFFAIR
Beautiful hairstyles could take hours to do and would therefore be an opportunity for some quality family time, bringing families together.

HIMBA TRIBE, NAMIBIA

The Himba tribe live in Namibia's Namib desert, and their hair is still used to communicate with other members of the tribe.

HAMAR TRIBE, ETHIOPIA

The Hamar tribe live in Ethiopia's Omo Valley. Hamar women wear thin locs in their hair called goscha and often feature colourful beaded jewellery.

CAPTIVITY HAIR

In 1444, white slave traders from Europe kidnapped African people from different tribes, regions and social classes. These Europeans knew hair was important to African people and decided to stop them from creating their amazing hairstyles by cutting off their hair. Thankfully the styles live on and are still worn by many today.

HEADWRAPS

In parts of America during the 18th century, Black women were legally required to cover their hair in public with fabric. Black women protested by buying BEAUTIFUL fabrics to use as headwraps, tying them in creative ways or adding jewels.

BLACK HAIR ICONS

JOSEPHINE BAKER

Josephine Baker was a civil rights activist and the first-ever Black woman to star in a major motion picture. Her beautiful sleek hairstyle was seen by Black women all over the world and became an iconic style.

BOB MARLEY

Bob Marley was a pioneer bringing wonderful Jamaican music to the world. He wore his hair in traditional Rastafarian locs.

CICELY TYSON

In 1963 actress Cicely Tyson became iconic as the first-ever Black woman to wear cornrows on television. She wore them in a famous American drama called *East Side/West Side*.

WILL SMITH

In the 1990s Will Smith helped to show the world high-top haircuts, like this one!

16

DIANA ROSS

Diana Ross became one of the most successful musicians of all time, so it was very powerful for her to embrace her afro in front of the world. Afros became a symbol of Black power, with the 'Black is Beautiful' movement in the 1960s.

KNOW YOUR TEXTURE

The beauty of afro hair is that it is truly unique and curl patterns can vary from crown to crown. It comes in many different textures.

WHAT ARE THE DIFFERENT HAIR TEXTURES?

Many people define hair texture by a number system. The system goes like this:

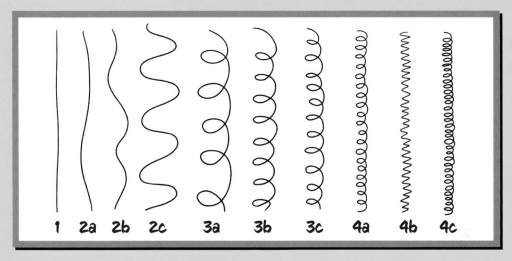

| 1 | 2a | 2b | 2c | 3a | 3b | 3c | 4a | 4b | 4c |

Type 1 is straight, type 2 is wavy, type 3 is curly and type 4 is coily. All types are beautiful! Knowing which hair type you have can help you when buying products for your hair, working out how much moisture you need and deciding how often you need to wash it. Afro textured hair most commonly falls into types 3 and 4.

HOW DO YOU LOOK AFTER YOUR HAIR TEXTURE?

Textured hair needs a lot more moisture than straight hair because moisture from your scalp doesn't travel to the ends of your hair easily. You may need to protect your hair from losing moisture at night by wearing a headscarf or bonnet.

HAIR CARE TIPS

We asked real-life Cocoa Girls for their top hair care tips:

"USE A TWIST HAIR BUTTER AT NIGHT TO LOCK IN THE MOISTURE AND TO DEFINE YOUR CURLS."

"ALWAYS KEEP YOUR HAIR WELL GREASED AND MOISTURISED."

"MAKE SURE YOU DON'T USE HEAT OR STRAIGHTEN YOUR HAIR TOO OFTEN."

"ALWAYS PLAIT YOUR HAIR IN THE EVENING IF IT HAS BEEN OUT ALL DAY, SO IT DOESN'T GET KNOTS."

"GET REGULAR TREATMENTS AND TRIMS SO YOUR HAIR CAN GROW."

"TRY TO KEEP STILL WHEN MUMMY IS DOING YOUR HAIR."

HOW TO SECTION AFRO HAIR

Sectioning is a vital step in creating so many different fun dos – learn the basics here.

STEP 1

With a wide-tooth comb to hand, begin by gently detangling the tresses before you do any sectioning or styling.

STEP 2

Start by sectioning larger parts of the hair with your comb. For example: divide the hair into two even parts and then four.

STEP 3

Once you feel comfortable creating large partings, experiment with smaller sections, which can help you create different-layered styles.

STEP 4

Now that you have divided the hair into several sections, work with a fine-tooth comb to straighten up the lines between each parting.

Now try sectioning in a heart shape.

STEP 1

Using a fine-tooth comb, create a square-shaped parting in the top front section of the hair and secure with a snag-free hairband.

STEP 2

Next, taking a small piece of hair, start to form the top of the heart-shaped section using the same comb. Then join these two sections of hair together and tie with a snag-free hairband.

STEP 3

Starting from the top of the middle section, use your comb to create a curved parting – from top-to-bottom – on both sides to form your heart-shaped section. Use snag-free hairbands to separate each section of hair and style with twists or braids as desired.

HOW TO DETANGLE THE HAIR

Detangle by misting your hair with water and adding lots of leave-in conditioner. Separate tangles gently with your fingers from your tips to roots, then use a wide-tooth comb.

BANTU KNOTS

BACK VIEW

24

STEP 1

Using a fine-tooth comb, section off the bottom third of your hair and separate into three sections. Secure with snag-free hairbands.

STEP 2

With the top two thirds of your hair, create a further six sections from the centre of the crown to the bottom and secure.

STEP 2

If you have sectioned the top part correctly it will create a star shape on top as shown.

STEP 3

Take each section and twist the hair tightly, starting at the top and working your way to the end.

USE GOLD ACCESSORIES TO DECORATE

STEP 4

Let the knot naturally curl and tuck the end near to the base of the hair with a bobby pin.

STEP 5

Once your Bantu knots are secured in place, add accessories or sparkly textures.

BANTU KNOTS
CONTINUED ...

SOUTH AFRICA

ZULU TRIBE

The Zulu tribe, who created the 'Bantu' or 'Zulu' knot, mainly lived in the KwaZulu-Natal province in South Africa.

KWAZULU-NATAL

DID YOU KNOW?

The word Bantu is used to describe the 300 to 600 ethnic groups within Southern Africa. The word Bantu means 'people'.

FRO-HAWK

FRONT VIEW

"
I love my hair
as it has so many
textures
"

28

STEP 1

Using a fine-tooth comb, section the hair horizontally into four even sections.

STEP 2

With a soft brush to hand, slick down the strands in each section from root-to-tip.

STEP 3

Starting from the top, pull the hair in each of the four sections up into a loose bun and secure with a snag-free hairband.

STEP 4

For smooth and sleek edges, apply a small amount of styling gel to each section as you move down the crown.

BACK VIEW

STEP 5

Unravel the bun in each section and finger-comb the tresses in an upward motion to finish.

MORE FRO-HAWKS

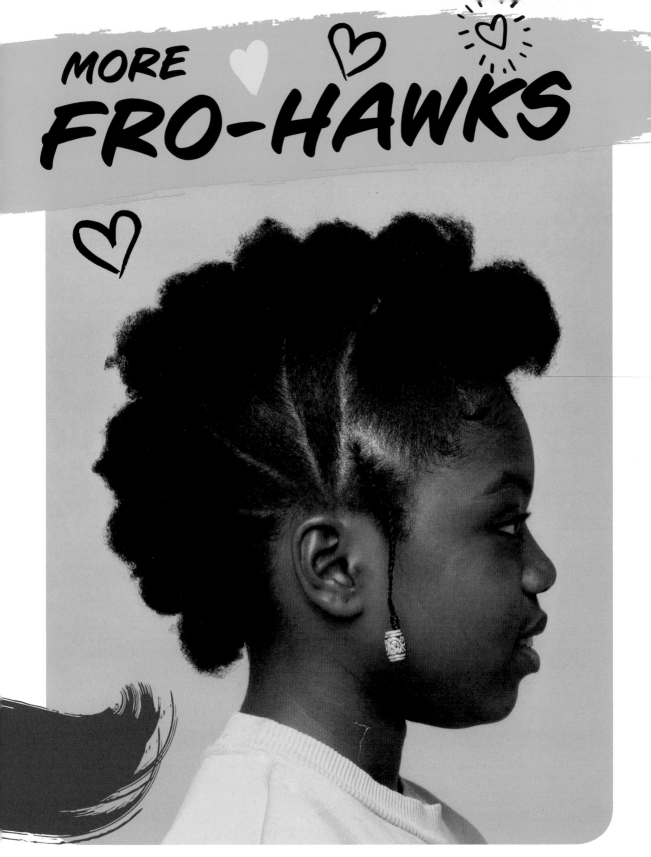

HOW TO
CORNROW

Learning how to cornrow gives you a great foundation for creating many different styles.

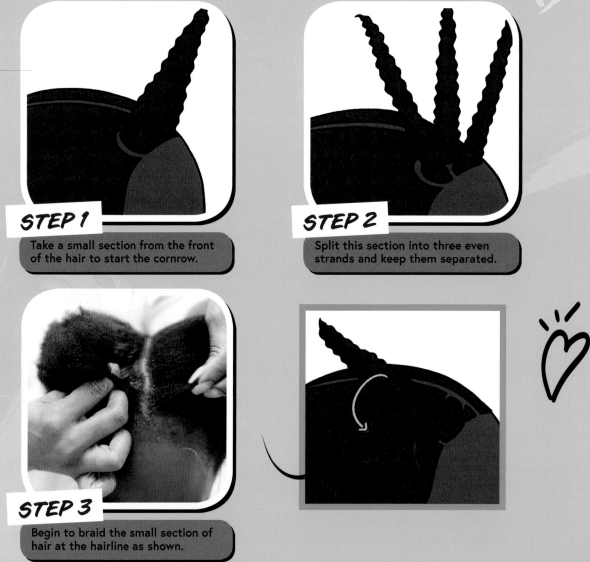

STEP 1

Take a small section from the front of the hair to start the cornrow.

STEP 2

Split this section into three even strands and keep them separated.

STEP 3

Begin to braid the small section of hair at the hairline as shown.

STEP 4

As you braid, add hair from the section you're braiding into the cornrow. To secure the cornrow onto the scalp, gently pull the hair as you pick up one of the three strands to braid.

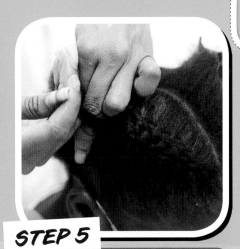

STEP 5

Continue to cornrow until you reach the tail of the braid and repeat steps 1 to 4 on other sections to complete the look.

WITH A BIT OF PRACTICE, YOU CAN DO STYLES AS AWESOME AS THIS!

FAITH'S
FEED-IN BRAIDS

> My hair is worthy of celebration

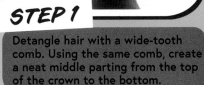

STEP 1

Detangle hair with a wide-tooth comb. Using the same comb, create a neat middle parting from the top of the crown to the bottom.

STEP 2

Before adding in the colour hair extensions, take a small section of natural hair and begin cornrowing for about three to four stitches.

STEP 3

Now that you've started the cornrow, it's time to add in your hair extensions. Place the loop of the hair extensions in the middle underneath the braid. Join one part of the hair extensions with the middle strand in the cornrow and the other part with the left strand.

STEP 4

With the hair extensions in position, continue to cornrow as normal while adding in more hair as you move down using the same application method in step 3.

STEP 5

As you come to the end of the cornrow, continue to plait the hair until you reach the tail of the braid. Secure with beads and small elastic bands.

EXPERIMENT WITH COLOUR

YOU CAN ALSO ADD RIBBONS TO THE END OF THE BRAIDS

* Faith is currently wearing her hair in this style to protect it, which is helping her hair grow.

HOW TO ADD BEADS

"I love how my hair swings and clicks to the rhythm of my beads"

STEP 1

Pick your favourite colourful or patterned beads and add them to your beading needle.

STEP 2

Next, hold your beading needle upright ready to apply the beads to your chosen hairstyle.

STEP 3

Place the beading needle at the tail of your braid and carefully pull the end of the hair through the eye.

STEP 4

Pull the needle over the beads and feed them into the braid and repeat until you have your desired look.

TRY ADDING DIFFERENT NUMBERS OF BEADS

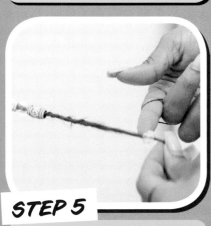

STEP 5

You can use an elastic band at the end of each braid to secure your beads in place.

LOVE IS IN the HAIR

SIDE VIEW

STEP 1

Section the hair horizontally into two large parts from ear to ear.

STEP 2

Create another parting from the centre of the crown to the bottom.

STEP 3

Next, get a fine-tooth comb and carefully form a parting in the shape of a heart.

STEP 4

Make two cornrows at the top of the parting and create a secondary heart-shaped parting below.

STEP 5

Once the heart is finished, you can create a cornrow style of your choice around the heart.

STEP 6

To finish the look, add a full set of different-coloured beads to the bottom of the braids.

EXPERIMENT WITH BEADS

TRY ADDING THE HEART SHAPE TO DIFFERENT STYLES!

39

HALO BRAID

FRONT VIEW

STEP 1

Create a large circle in the middle of the head, leaving the hair around the front of the face to form a separate section.

STEP 2

Divide the larger section into five parts to cornrow. Start the cornrow at the crown and work your way out, leaving the ends loose.

STEP 3

Next, create the halo braid from the front section of hair, making sure it weaves into the smaller cornrows as you move along.

STEP 4

Continue to cornrow the halo braid until you reach full-circle at the bottom of the crown and secure it with a bobby pin.

STEP 5

Finally, cornrow the front section of the hair on both sides of the face to frame the halo braid.

HAIR PUFFS

STEP 1

To start the style, section the hair into four parts from the top-centre to the bottom, and from ear to ear across the middle of the crown.

STEP 2

Using a styling gel and a comb, smooth down the edges of the hair in an upward motion and start to cornrow the top two sections.

STEP 3

Now that the cornrows are complete, take a wide-tooth comb and gently brush out the two bottom sections of the hair for extra volume.

STEP 4

Finally, gather the hair up into two loose buns – while tucking the braid tail away – and secure the style with snag-free hairbands.

SIDE VIEW

BACK VIEW

HAIR PUFFS
CONTINUED ...

LION MANE ♡ PONYTAIL

STEP 1

Using a fine-tooth comb, create a small section in the middle of the crown and secure in place with a snag-free hairband.

STEP 2

Next, pull the remaining hair – around the centre piece – into a ponytail and secure it in place with another elastic band. For super-sleek edges, use a soft brush to smooth down hair and style the baby hairs.

STEP 3

Finally, use a wide-tooth comb to brush out the ponytail and add extra volume.

FLORAL 'FRO

STEP 1

Begin by detangling your hair using a wide-tooth comb and add moisture with a styling serum.

STEP 2

Pick up your floral accessory of choice and place it where you want it in your hair.

STEP 3

Using a bobby pin, secure the floral hair accessory in place.

STEP 4

If you want to add more, repeat steps 2 to 3 to get the desired look.

> **My hair bounces with joy and pride**

EXPERIMENT WITH DIFFERENT FLOWERS

47

TWISTED UPDO

STEP 1

Section the hair into three main parts in the front, middle and back using a fine-tooth comb. Leave two side strands for the braids that hang down at the end.

STEP 2

Starting at the front of your hair, take your first section and separate it into smaller hexagonal sections and secure them using elastic bands.

STEP 3

Continue to work through the front section until it is fully secured with elastic bands.

STEP 4

Now move onto the back section of the hair and repeat steps 2 to 3.

STEP 5

Continue to tightly secure each strand in place with an elastic band – while slightly pulling the hair – as you work through this section.

STEP 6

Choose a set of beads to style the hair with. Once you are ready, start to feed one set of beads into the base of the hair.

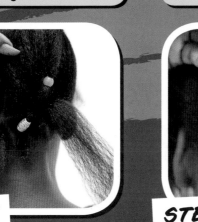

STEP 7

Continue to add a second set of beads to the hair, leaving a 5cm gap between both.

STEP 8

Weave each of your beaded sections over one another in a pattern. Secure with elastic bands.

STEP 9

Now, repeat steps 6 to 8 to style the front section of the hair adding beads and creating a pattern that will sit on the crown of your head.

STEP 10

Split the middle section into two parts. Twist the front part with the ends of the beaded hair until your hair starts to naturally curl into a knot and then pin in place.

49

STEP 11

Next, take the back part and repeat the process of twisting and pinning the knots as you move down.

STEP 12

Brush the loose ends of the hair through with your fingers to detangle as you work your way from the middle to the bottom.

STEP 13

Take the two loose strands on either side and tie with an elastic band at the top and then twist the hair to the bottom.

STEP 14

Go back over the updo to make sure all of the knots are secured in place before adding any desired final touches.

STEP 15

Finally, finish up by adding styling gel to the edges and beads to the ends of the twists.

51

My hair is unique and special

53

GLITTER HAIR

STEP 1

Divide the front of the hair into six sections and create cornrows with colourful hair extensions using the feed-in method from page 38.

STEP 2

Close the cornrow at the centre of the crown and then continue to braid the hair freely until you reach the end of your feed-in texture.

STEP 3

Twist the braided ends into Bantu knots and then pin them into place using a bobby pin. For our full Bantu knots tutorial, turn to page 28.

STEP 4

Using a makeup brush, add a touch of glitter hair gel to either side of your colour cornrows to make this hairstyle sparkle!

* Be very careful not to get glitter gel anywhere near your eyes or mouth.

COCOA HAIR GALLERY

> **My hair is fierce and brave, soft and gentle**

57

> **66** My hair is the perfect halo for my head **99**

61

63

I LOVE MY HAIR BECAUSE...

" ... every single curly, kinky coil is filled with love. "

" ... it's mine, it was given to me and tells a story of my history.

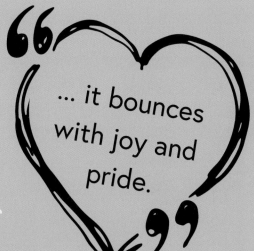

" ... it bounces with joy and pride.

" ... it's my heritage and legacy. From where I came to where I am going to be. "

THANK YOU!

TO ALL THE COCOA GIRLS AND BOYS WHO HELPED TO MAKE THIS BOOK

HAIR MODELS
Faith
Tallulah
Sonia
Prisca
Emilia
Sonia
Sienna
Soriaya
Aviana
Isabella
Nia
Paige
Tyiana
Taiya
Zariah
Maya
Ava H
Luiciana
Sarah
Carma
Jasmin-Rae
Zara
Ava Rae
Kelani
Chloe
Chance
Naima
Tyrenae
Fyna
Acacia
Nile
Dior

HAIRSTYLISTS
Jasmin Clarke (Hey Bambino)
Dionne Smith
Chantel (Mini Manes)
November Love
Lorraine Dublin
Kimberley Taylor (The Curl Clinic)
Lavinia (Sleek Braiding)
Shikira Daley (Styles by Shak's)
Raquel Ndoye

PHOTOGRAPHERS
Boyd Visuals
Condry Calvin Mlilo
Shanin @ The Little Pop-Up
Lol Johnson

STYLISTS
Kelis Africa
Denise Brown
Yvadney